Another Mouse to Feed

by Robert Kraus
pictures by Jose Aruego & Ariane Dewey

Prentice-Hall Books for Young Readers
A Division of Simon & Schuster, Inc.
New York

Text copyright © 1980 by Simon & Schuster, Inc.
Illustrations copyright © 1980 by Jose Aruego and Ariane Dewey

First Printing by Prentice-Hall Books for Young Readers, 1987

Prentice-Hall Books for Young Readers
A Division of Simon & Schuster, Inc.
Simon & Schuster Building
Rockefeller Center
1230 Avenue of the Americas
New York, NY 10020

Prentice-Hall Books for Young Readers
is a trademark of Simon & Schuster, Inc.

Designed by The Etheredges
Manufactured in the United States of America

10 9 8 7 6 5 4 3 2 1

10 9 8 7 6 5 4 3 2 1 pbk

Library of Congress Cataloging in Publication Data
Kraus, Robert, Another mouse to feed.
SUMMARY: When Mr. and Mrs. Mouse became exhausted from overwork,
caring for their many children, the little mice decide to take over.
[1. Mice—Fiction. 2. Parent and child—Fiction] I. Aruego, Jose. II. Dewey, Ariane.
III. Title. PZ7.K868 An [E] 78-21259
ISBN 0-13-036930-6
ISBN 0-13-036922-5 pbk

Mr. and Mrs. Mouse had many children,
so many in fact that they often forgot their names,
as well as how many they had.

To help make ends meet, Mrs. Mouse got a job as a roller skating instructor. It was a lot of work, but she never complained because she loved little mice, especially her own.

It was a lot of work for Mr. Mouse too.
In fact, he had to have three jobs to earn enough
money to take care of his family, but he didn't mind,
because he too, loved little mice,
especially his own.

"I have my hands full with all these mice,"
said **Mrs. Mouse**.
"I think our family is big enough."

"I don't think I could manage four jobs,"
said **Mr. Mouse**.
"I think our family is big enough, too."

They were just having a cup of tea, when
there was a knock on the door.

"Who could it be at this time of night?" asked
Mrs. Mouse.

"There's one way to find out," said Mr. Mouse,
and he opened the door. And on the doorstep
was a wicker basket containing a tiny mouse, wrapped
in a blanket. A note was pinned to the blanket,
reading: "Take care of my child."

"A mouse in need..." said Mrs. Mouse,

"...is another mouse to feed," said Mr. Mouse.

All the mouse children were delighted. It was
nice to meet a mouse who wasn't a brother or a sister.

Mrs. Mouse went to the employment agency to get a second job.

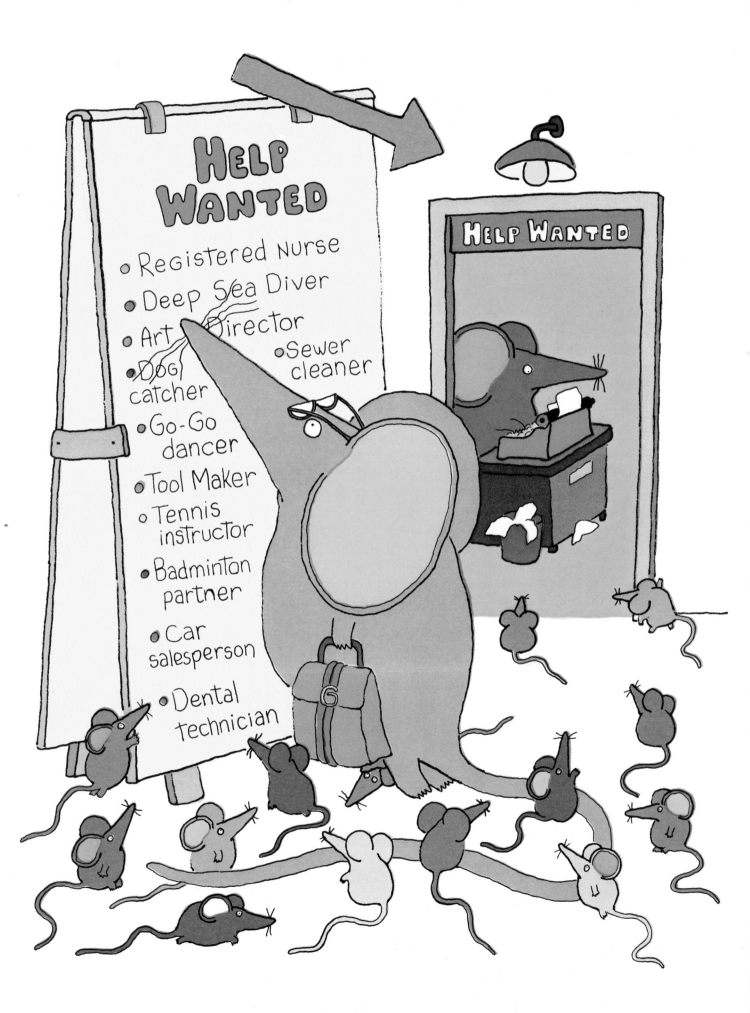

At home, Mr. Mouse started scrubbing clean clothes
and stirring empty pots. They were both cracking up.

Edgar, the oldest child, noticed it first,
and he told the others.

"If two parents can support thirty-one children,
then thirty-two children can support two parents,"
Edgar declared. "Dad, you take a much-needed
vacation from your jobs. Mom, you forget
about teaching roller skating for now. Your children
are going to take over."

"But what about your education?" asked Mrs. Mouse.

"We'll work after school, weekends and holidays," said Edgar.

So all the mouse children who were old enough, got after-school jobs,

and those who weren't old enough to go to school,
did housework and took care of the new mouse.

Edgar, modeling himself after his father
got two after-school jobs: delivering newspapers

and sweeping up in a grocery store.

And with seventeen mice cleaning house, it was spotless; with fourteen mice working, the money was soon rolling in.

Edgar kept it in cookie jars.
He spent what was needed for necessities and
saved what was left for a rainy day.

Soon, Mr. Mouse and Mrs. Mouse were rested and eager to get back to work. "I'd go nuts just sitting around," said Mr. Mouse.

Mr. Mouse became a Fireman

and Mrs. Mouse became a tennis instructor.

Mr. and Mrs. Mouse also began scrubbing, cleaning and cooking again.

But sometimes they just sat down and enjoyed their children.

All the mouse children continued their after-school
jobs because they enjoyed working, and the
extra money helped.

Before long, Baby Mouse was helping, too.